ArtScroll

GEMARAKUP
Super Sleuth
1

MEET
GEMARAKUP

by Miriam Stark Zakon

Mesorah Publications, ltd

FIRST EDITION
First Impression … June 1990
SECOND EDITION
First Impression … July 2003
Third Impression … February 2012

Published and Distributed by
MESORAH PUBLICATIONS, LTD.
4401 Second Avenue / Brooklyn, N.Y 11232

Distributed in Europe by
LEHMANNS
Unit E, Viking Industrial Park
Rolling Mill Road NE32 3DP
Jarow, Tyne & Wear,
England

Distributed in Australia and New Zealand
by **GOLDS WORLD OF JUDAICA**
3-13 William Street
Balaclava, Melbourne 3183
Victoria Australia

Distributed in Israel by
SIFRIATI / A. GITLER BOOKS
6 Hayarkon Street
Bnei Brak 51127

Distributed in South Africa by
KOLLEL BOOKSHOP
Shop 8A Norwood Hypermarket
Norwood 2196, Johannesburg, South Africa

ARTSCROLL YOUTH SERIES®
GEMARAKUP SUPER SLEUTH SERIES®
BOOK 1 – MEET GEMARAKUP
© *Copyright 1990, by MESORAH PUBLICATIONS, Ltd.*
4401 Second Avenue / Brooklyn, N.Y. 11232 / (718) 921-9000 / www.artscroll.com

---

Typography by CompuScribe at ArtScroll Studios, Ltd.

Manufactured in the United States of America by Noble Book Press Corp.

Table of Contents

Meet Gemarakup

t last, after many short winter days and long winter nights, *Chanukah* was finally at hand. The class was given time off for an informal party in the last fifteen minutes of school, before vacation officially began. And those two good friends, Yisrael David and Nachman Moshe, were busy exchanging the gifts they'd bought each other with their *Chanukah gelt*.

Yisrael David eagerly tore at the envelope. "Wow!" he exclaimed. "Two Rav Moshes, the Steipler, and the Satmar Rebbe! How'd you know I was missing these from my collection, Slugger?"

Nachman Moshe — alias "Slugger" to everyone who knew him (except his *rebbe* and his mother), because of his love for

baseball — shrugged. "You know I don't understand why you collect *gedolim* cards," he said, "but I knew you would like them. And what have we here?"

He tugged at the large package that Yisrael David — alias "Gemarakup" to everyone (except, you guessed it, his *rebbe* and his mother), because of his sharp mind and excellence in learning — had given him. He opened the box and pulled out wad after wad of newspaper. Inside, he finally found a small envelope.

"Great!" he cried. "A Goodwin, a Brown, and a Martino! Terrific!"

Gemarakup grinned. "You know I think baseball cards are dopey, Slugger — but I knew that you wanted them."

When the last bell had rung, and all the goodbyes had finally been said, the two friends — the two brightest boys in the entire sixth grade of Yeshiva Ahavas Chesed — walked home together.

"What are you doing for vacation?" asked Slugger.

"Tonight is Chezky's party," answered Gemarakup. "And tomorrow morning, we're traveling to Baltimore. I've got to start packing as soon as I get home."

"Be sure to take all the *gedolim* cards," his friend teased him.

"Oh, I can leave them at home," said Gemarakup with a smile. "After all, I always have my stories."

You see, Gemarakup's "collection" of tales and stories about *tzaddikim,* scholars, and sages was even bigger than his collection of *gedolim* cards. He "collected" them from his parents, from his *rebbeim,* from youth leaders, and from books; he would hear them, remember them, and tell them over and over again. Grownups thought they were fantastic, but Slugger was not impressed.

"Oh, your stories," he groaned. "You'd be better off with a baseball bat."

But, as it turned out, Slugger was to be proven wrong, and very, very soon.

I.
The Unlucky Dreidel

"Go, dreidel, go!" cried Slugger.

"C'mon, I need a *gimmel*," muttered Chezky.

Five boys sat intently around the dining-room table, staring at the large pile of coins gleaming before them. They rubbed their *dreidels*, pleaded with them, or practiced spinning them upside down, while they awaited their turns.

Slugger, Chezky, Avi, Yehudah, and Leib each spun. And, once again, it was Slugger who came out on top, with a *gimmel*.

"What a *dreidel*!" he gloated as he pulled the heap of coins toward him.

"I can't understand it!" murmured Chezky. "He wins every time!" He stared at his own *dreidel,* which was the same size and color as his adversary's. "Why don't you do some winning for a change?" he grumbled to it.

"Time out!" Gemarakup announced, pushing a wheeled cart in front of him. "Come and get your *latkes,* drowning in oil."

Mrs. Schwartz, Chezky's mother, followed him in. "Chezky, I've got boiled potato *pirogen* for you. Chezky is allergic to foods fried in oil," she explained to the other boys.

They all put down their *dreidels* and turned their attention to the food, finishing off the *latkes* without even waiting for Mrs. Schwartz to bring plastic forks and knives. When the last *latke* had been eaten, they resumed their game, with Slugger continuing his winning streak. Soon after, Chezky's mother called them into the kitchen for one last treat — *sufganiyot,* the deep-fried jelly donut that Israelis eat on *Chanukah.* Chezky, because of his allergy, ate special *dreidel*-shaped cookies, baked just for the occasion.

When they returned to the living room, they found the *dreidels* neatly arranged in a row on the table, with Chezky's four-year-old brother Ephraim happily surveying his handiwork. With a scowl at his little brother, Chezky gave each *dreidel* back to its owner, and the game began once again. Gemarakup, though, refused to join, preferring to read a biography of Rav Yosef Karo.

"C'mon, Gemarakup," his friend Slugger urged, "you've just got to watch me win some more!"

Gemarakup just shook his head in refusal, and turned back to his book.

Minutes later, though, his concentration was broken by a shout at the table. "Lost again! Something's wrong here!"

"What's happening, Slugger?" asked Gemarakup.

"Fishy business is what's happening," said Slugger. "Until we stopped for *sufganiyot,* my *dreidel* never stopped on a *shin* or a *nun.* I couldn't lose."

"Must have been weighted improperly," said Gemarakup thoughtfully.

"I don't care why. It was a lucky *dreidel!* But then we stopped for jelly donuts — and now I've lost my luck. Someone else has gotten my good luck and my *dreidel,*" he said, glaring at Chezky. "It must have gotten mixed up with another one when Ephraim was fooling around with them."

"Did not," declared Chezky hotly. "We both had red *dreidels.* You can't prove that this one belongs to you. Maybe your luck just ran out!"

"It's mine!" shouted Slugger angrily.

"Hold on a minute," said Gemarakup, after a moment's thought. "I've got a way to prove if the *dreidel* belongs to Chezky or Slugger. And all I need is a cup of water!"

Can you figure out how Gemarakup will find the true owner of the lucky *dreidel*? [Turn to page 59 for the solution.]

II.
The Great Jewel Robbery

omething was wrong in the Finkel home.

The toast was burned, the eggs were raw, the chocolate was missing from the milk.

Something was terribly wrong. You didn't have to be a Gemarakup to deduce that.

"What's the matter today, *Imma?*" asked the eldest son of the Finkel family, Yisrael David — known as Gemarakup to his friends — wrinkling his nose as he bit into the charred toast.

"I'm sorry, *Tattele,* I'm a bit rattled this morning," his mother replied. She hastily smeared peanut butter on a slice of bread destined for a tuna fish sandwich, noticed her mistake, and ruefully reached for the jelly instead. "I had some worrying news this morning."

"Is something wrong?" piped up eight-year-old Tamar.

"Oh, nothing terribly serious," their mother reassured them. "Uncle Ezra just called with some upsetting news. He's been robbed!"

"Robbed?" Gemarakup tried to keep the excitement out of his voice and sound solemn, but failed. A real robbery! For a long time, he'd had a hunch that he could apply his knowledge of Jewish learning and tales to solve problems. The difficulty was that so few problems seemed to come his way. And now, a robbery!

"What happened?" he asked.

"He didn't tell me much over the phone. A man came into his store and asked to see a valuable diamond ring. When Uncle Ezra brought it out onto the counter, the man pulled out a gun, grabbed the ring, and ran out. Uncle Ezra immediately pressed a hidden button to sound an alarm, and the police caught the man as he was driving away."

"The police caught him? So what's the trouble? The robber goes to jail, the diamond is returned, and Uncle Ezra is a hero."

"Not exactly. You see, they couldn't find the diamond."

"Couldn't find the diamond?" Gemarakup echoed incredulously.

"That's right. They searched the man, searched the car, the store, and the entire area. No diamond. And to make matters worse, it was a one-of-a-kind stone, a very valuable one."

Mrs. Finkel glanced at the clock. "Oh, no! Eight o'clock already! You'll miss your buses if you don't fly out of here right now! You don't need sweaters," she added, looking out the window. "It looks like another beautiful, sunny day. A whole week in November without rain. I wonder how long this spring-like weather will last?"

Gemarakup was the last to go slamming out the door. As he left, he turned and shouted to his mother: "Can I visit Uncle Ezra after school, *Imma?* I want to cheer him up."

Mrs. Finkel nodded her assent, and watched her son go bounding down the steps." It'll take more than a favorite nephew to cheer up my brother," she thought to herself. "What he needs is a Sherlock Holmes to solve his mystery."

Which just goes to show that even a mother can sometimes underestimate her son.

When Gemarakup walked into his uncle's store after school that afternoon, he found a sign on the door announcing that it was closed. He peered in beneath the shades covering the windows, and saw someone moving around. Anxiously, he pounded on the door.

Uncle Ezra himself answered. "Oh, it's you," he said, somewhat ungraciously.

Gemarakup displayed his most winning smile. "May I come in, Uncle Ezra?" he asked.

Uncle Ezra hesitated, and then shrugged. "Sure. But be very quiet, the police are here."

A man dressed in a plain gray suit, a detective, was leaning against a counter, carefully watching two uniformed policemen searching the premises. Uncle Ezra and Gemarakup stood quietly in a corner, watching their progress — or lack of it.

Finally, the two policemen reported to the detective, "Sorry, sir, we've found nothing at all."

"I can't understand it. He had no time to get rid of it," said Uncle Ezra, despair in his voice.

The plainclothesman spoke for the first time. "Let's take a look at the videotape again."

"We've got closed-circuit televisions monitoring the store all the time," Uncle Ezra explained to Gemarakup, as the policeman set up a small viewer. "The robbery was actually filmed. I've looked at it a dozen times, but I can't see where he dumped the diamond."

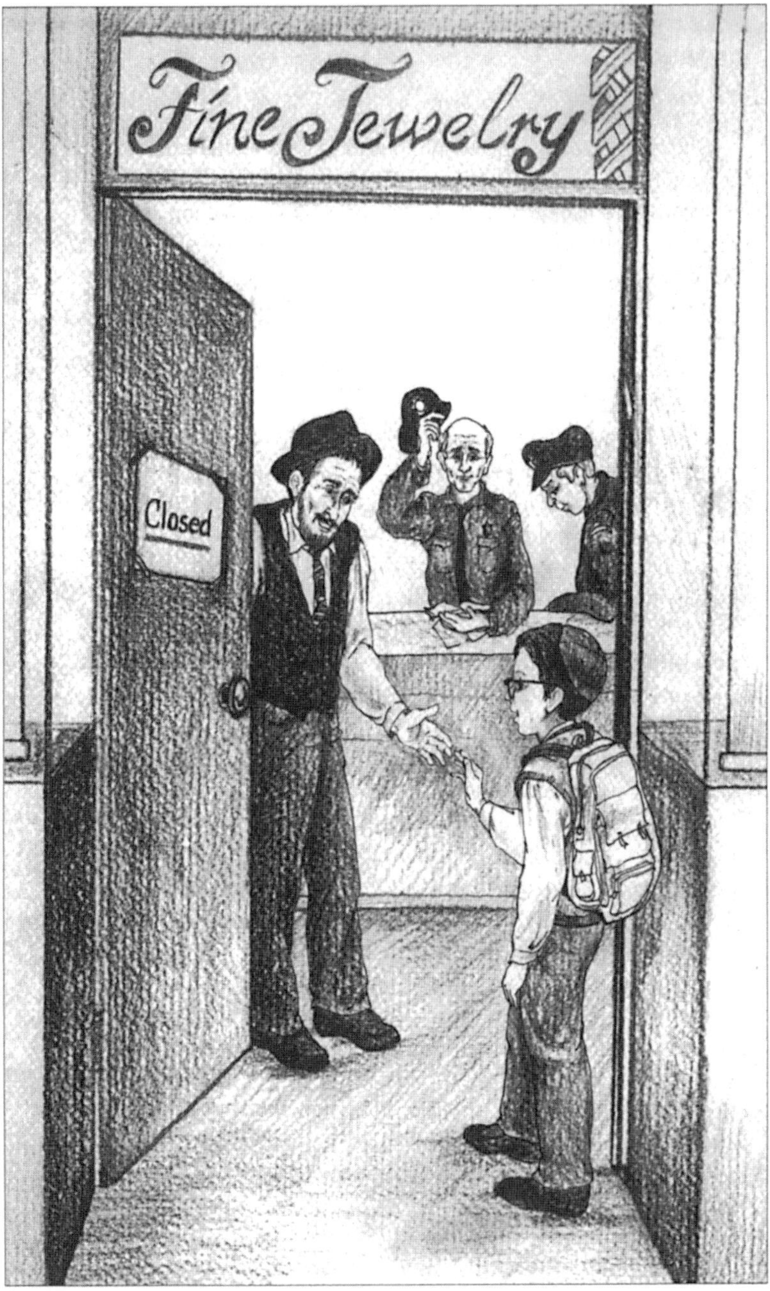
Fine Jewelry
Closed

Soon, Gemarakup was watching the flickering images on the screen. He saw Ezra standing behind the counter, with a salesman next to him. Two customers were also present, an elderly woman choosing a gold bracelet and a young man in a dark suit carrying an umbrella. The door opened, and a swarthy, heavyset man walked in. He spoke to Ezra, who took out a black box and opened it, displaying an enormous diamond. The man reached into his pocket and pulled out a snub-nosed revolver. He grabbed the diamond, turned, and fled out of the store, shoving the young man with the umbrella and knocking the elderly woman to the ground.

The videotape ended. All were silent.

"You see," Ezra finally said. "Not a clue in sight."

"Not exactly," replied Gemarakup. "There is a clue, and it is in plain sight, and if we're lucky, it will lead us directly to the diamond."

Can you spot the clue that Gemarakup saw? Turn to page 62 for the solution.

III.

The Bad-Tempered Kohein

n the sixth grade class of Yeshiva Ahavas Chesed, the subject was *Kohanim*.

"Name some of the situations where a *Kohein* has a different *halachah* from others," the *rebbe* asked.

There was a flurry of answers.

"He was allowed to eat from certain *korbanos.*"

"He received the *terumah*."

"He didn't own land in *Eretz Yisrael.*"

The *rebbe* nodded. "You are all correct," he said. "But what about today? Are there any times when we treat a *Kohein* differently, now that we have no *Beis Hamikdash?*"

Gemarakup's hand quickly shot up into the air — and just as quickly came down, as he felt a sharp jab between his shoulder blades.

"Pssst," whispered his best friend, Slugger. "Can you come over today after school? I want to get started on that history project."

Gemarakup motioned to Slugger to be quiet. He wanted to hear what the *rebbe* had to say.

Slugger, unfortunately, was more interested in his friend's attention — and so, moments later, he delivered another jab to Gemarakup's back.

Gemarakup resigned himself to the inevitable, and quickly whispered an answer to his friend. He finished just in time to hear his *rebbe's* answer. And so it was he, and not his good friend, Slugger, who learned that day how to solve the problem of the bad-tempered *Kohein*.

❈ ❈ ❈

As the two friends made their way towards Slugger's house, eagerly discussing the map they planned to make, they heard the sound of raised voices. They turned a corner and found two of their classmates, Chaim Cohen and Pinchas Katz, ready to fly at each other. They were held back only by the strong restraining arms of two eighth graders, each of whom held one of them securely in a tight grip.

A small crowd had already collected to hear the boys trade insults.

"Everyone knows you're the cowardliest, creepiest *kvetch* of the entire school," shouted Chaim.

"You — you brainless bully of a nincompoop!" retorted Pinchas.

"What happened?" asked Gemarakup, as both boys paused to catch their breaths.

A third grader who was enjoying the interplay of insults answered breathlessly, "Pinchas was running and knocked into Chaim, who says he did it on purpose."

"Clumsy oaf!" "Idiot!" The insults were getting louder, with the two ignoring the older boys' advice to calm down.

"Cohen and Katz, huh." Gemarakup's eyes lit up, and he

said, almost to himself, "It's worth a try."

He walked into the middle of the fray. "Hey, guys, if you want to fight — fight. But do it right."

The two combatants stopped short. Clearly, this was not what they expected to hear from the class "brain."

"We can't have common brawling here, near the school," continued Gemarakup coolly. "We'll make it a proper fight." He turned to Slugger and said, "Your brother has boxing gloves, doesn't he?"

His friend nodded, astonished.

"Pinchas, go with Slugger, and get the gloves."

There was a ring of command in his voice that they couldn't ignore; the two boys set off at a fast clip.

"You, Chaim. We need a boxing ring. Go find some rope — fast!"

He, too, raced away, returning breathless, with two jump ropes. "My sister said we could use these!"

"Now, string them up. Attach them to that pole. Quick, now."

Gemarakup's instructions came out swiftly and surely, and the panting boy had soon set up an impromptu boxing ring.

"While we wait for the gloves, let's get you in training," said Gemarakup. "Run around the ring a few times."

Minutes passed as the bystanders watched the strange sight. Just as Chaim began to slow down, Slugger and Pinchas raced back, panting.

"Good," cried Gemarakup. He slowly laced up the gloves on the two boys, who were doing their best to avoid each other's glances. At last Gemarakup led the two, gloved and still breathless, into the ring. "Now, we can do it properly. Fight!"

Pinchas raised his gloved hand, smiled just a little, and extended it to Chaim, who shook it slowly. The two boys grinned sheepishly at each other, and walked out of the ring together, clapping Gemarakup on the back. Soon, they had dis-

appeared out of sight, laughing together.

"Wow, what a strange way to end a fight," said Slugger to his friend. "Luckily, they saw how stupid they were being."

"Luck had nothing to do with it," Gemarakup replied. "I simply applied something we had all learned today in class."

Can you figure out what gave Gemarakup the clue to ending the fight? [Turn to page 63 for the solution.]

IV.
The Hungry Hoodlums

he basketball game in the *yeshiva* yard was put off for about an hour while all the boys sat on the school's stone steps and watched a small army of vehicles drive past the building. There were several bulldozers, a gigantic steam roller, and four dump trucks.

"They're going to tear up and rebuild the entire Green Street," Slugger told his friend Gemarakup. "The street will be closed for over a month. Motke told me; it's going to hurt his business terribly."

Motke was the owner of the kosher pizza shop that had recently opened next door to their *yeshiva*. Though they complained that it was "the greasiest joint this side of the ocean," the boys all liked the genial Israeli who had opened the eatery, and enjoyed having hot pizza so close to their school. Gemarakup hoped that the construction wouldn't do Motke too much harm.

The drivers parked their monstrous trucks and returned home, leaving them until morning, when construction would begin; the show was now over. The boys turned their attention back to the basketball game, with Gemarakup acting, as always, as referee.

Because of the delay in starting, it was already dark when the boys prepared to head home. Suddenly, they heard the sound of glass shattering.

"Someone's trying to break into the *yeshiva*," cried Gemarakup. He, Slugger, and several of the others sprinted towards the school's front entrance.

When they got there, they found four of the school's windows broken. The building's marble facade had been spray-painted with ugly phrases and anti-Semitic slogans.

They heard the pounding of feet on the pavement nearby, and raced after the retreating backs of four figures. The vandals, though, had too great a start, and even Slugger, fastest of the boys, couldn't keep up with them. They were soon lost to sight.

"Nothing we can do but call the police," said Yanky.

"Did you see them? Could you identify them?" Gemarakup asked Slugger.

"I only saw their backs," replied Slugger, frustration in his voice. "One of them was wearing a black leather jacket. That's all I saw. The police will never catch them, you'll see."

The boys flagged down a passing squad car, and showed the police officer the damage. He radioed for help, and, when another patrol car had come, spoke to the boys.

"Get in," he said, "and we'll ride around. Maybe we can spot the vandals."

Gemarakup, Slugger, and two of their friends jumped into the car. For over an hour they rode slowly through the area, looking for suspicious characters. Finally, the car turned towards the police precinct.

As they were approaching the parking lot, they noticed four boys nonchalantly walking down the street. One was wearing a black leather jacket.

"That's them — I think !" cried Slugger excitedly.

The police officer called the four over to the car. One of them, he noticed, had a can of spray paint jutting out of his jeans pocket.

"Come inside, boys," he commanded, pointing to the station. "We've got something to talk about."

A burly sergeant led them into a small room. When the four tough-looking youths were seated, the questioning began.

"What were you doing with the can of spray paint?"

The oldest boy, obviously the leader of the gang, replied, "Nuthin."

"Where were you tonight, about an hour ago?"

"In our neighborhood, near the park."

"Were you anywhere near the vicinity of Green Street and Fourth Avenue tonight?"

Another of the youths burst out, "We weren't doin' nuthin'! We ain't got nuthin' to do in that neighborhood, anyhow — we haven't been there for weeks!"

The sergeant turned to Slugger. "Can you positively identify any of them?"

Slugger stared hard, squirmed, and shrugged. "I'm sure it's them," he whispered to Gemarakup. "And yet ..."

He turned to the police officer. "I'm sorry, sir. It was dark, and we were all running. I think it's them, but I can't say so for certain."

"Well," said the sergeant, to the young toughs, "we can't hold you. You can go home."

Slugger and his friends threw angry glances at the youths, and turned to go. To their astonishment, however, Gemarakup walked over to them, and, with a cheerful smile, put his hand out.

"We're sorry to have put you through this," he said to the four unfriendly faces staring at him. "Tell you what — why don't you join us for pizza — our treat — just to show that there are no hard feelings? There's a kosher pizza shop — you know, we eat only kosher — not far from our school."

Before anyone could interrupt, the leader — who hadn't eaten for several hours — grinned broadly. "Sure," he said. "Your treat."

Gemarakup turned to the police officer. "Do you think you could possibly give us a lift to Green Street? We'd really appreciate it."

"You'll have to take another route," the leader said, as he donned his black leather jacket. "Green Street's closed for construction."

"Wait a minute, Sergeant," Gemarakup called. "These characters are lying — I can prove it."

Can you figure out how Gemarakup proved that the hoodlums had lied? [Turn to page 64 for the solution.]

V.
The Terror of Teaneck

very year, the Finkel clan had its family reunion, with all the children, grandchildren, aunts, uncles, nieces, and nephews gathering together for an evening of talk and food, and reminiscing and more food, and children's play and still more food. Tonight the gathering was being held, for the first time, in the tiny apartment of the most recent newlyweds in the family, Yehoshua Finkel and his wife Shoshana.

Yosh and Shosh, as they were known to almost everyone, stood at the door, greeting the new arrivals as they came down the corridor. *"Shalom, Shalom,"* Yosh said warmly to Rabbi and Mrs. Finkel, while fondly slapping their son on the back. Close behind them came the next guests, Aunt Leah and Uncle Yaakov, who had driven in from New Jersey. With them,

Gemarakup noted with a sigh, was their three-year-old son Benjy, the apple of his mother's eye, whom Gemarakup had privately come to nickname "The Terror of Teaneck." (Naturally, he never told anyone — Gemarakup, after all, knew all about the importance of avoiding *lashon hara!*)

"Just put your coats in the bedroom," Shosh told her newly arrived guests, "and come in for some hot drinks. You must be freezing."

Gemarakup casually dumped his warm winter jacket on the growing heap that was piled on Yosh's bed (small apartments don't have much closet space), and gratefully accepted the hot cup of tea handed to him. After he had said his hellos, he sat down and listened with half an ear to three of his uncles talking. The other part of his busy brain was taking in the scene: *Savta* was looking at the pictures of her youngest grandchild. His aunts were helping Shosh bring in tray after tray of beautifully arranged meats and salads. His younger sister Tamar and their cousin Libby were playing a game together in a corner. And Benjy was wolfing down a plate of potato chips, spilling soda on his cousin Aharon, feeding salami to the parakeet, making faces behind *Tante* Ida's back, quietly pouring himself an overflowing glass of vodka and guzzling some down, and not so quietly having a coughing fit — The Terror of Teaneck!

Benjy was duly slapped on the back, worried over, and scolded, and he soon disappeared sulkily under the table. Gemarakup then turned his attention fully to the conversation going on around him. His uncles were on the topic of *yeshivos* and were comparing those of the past, back in Europe, and the present ones in America.

"You must admit, Ezra, that even if the learning is more intense today, there is nothing like the sacrifice of the students back in European *yeshivos,*" said Uncle Dave.

"I'm not so sure of that," retorted Uncle Ezra, mostly because he enjoyed a good argument with his brother David. "After all, when everyone around you is poor, is it such a sacrifice to be poor, too?"

Here Gemarakup felt compelled to put in his opinion. "But Uncle Ezra, you have no idea how some of the *yeshiva* boys suffered in order to learn! They would eat one meal a day, and each day in a different home. They never knew where their next good meal would come from! And some of them were so poor that they slept in their unheated *beis midrash,* on benches! Why, I was just reading about the Steipler…"

"Help!" interrupted his cousin Shmuel, laughing. "We've got Gemarakup started on his stories; now, no one gets a chance to talk!"

Gemarakup, who often heard jokes about his hobby of collecting stories of *gedolim,* grinned good-naturedly, and — just to show his cousin! — refused to say another word.

He turned his attention to the mass of food that his *Tante* Ida had placed on his plate: a quarter of a chicken, two helpings of *kugel,* four slices of roast beef, three knishes, and a cup of soda. Later, Gemarakup leaned back in his chair with a sigh. With everyone eating, the room had grown quiet — too quiet, thought Gemarakup. "Hey, where's Benjy?" he asked conversationally.

"In the kitchen, I suppose," replied his mother. "Shosh — please send Benjy out for some food," she called.

Shosh stepped into the room, her hands full of platters of cake. "He's not in here," she said.

"Well, where is he?" said his father impatiently.

"I saw him last under the table," someone replied. Everyone duly looked under their chairs — no Benjy.

Aunt Leah looked worried. "I can't imagine where that child has gone to," she said. She opened the door to each room, calling his name — no answer.

The worried look appeared on more faces. Everyone, after all, knew that Benjy was the kind of child who might go anywhere, do anything.

Several voices spoke at once. "Check the hallway, maybe he walked out the door." "Are you certain he's not under the table?" "Benjy — oh, Benjy!" "Maybe we should notify the police."

Tears appeared in Aunt Leah's eyes.

Gemarakup stood to one side, thinking. For some reason, he felt that something that had been said tonight might be important. Wait — that's right! It could be!

Moments later, he appeared with a cherubic-faced boy sleeping in his arms. Aunt Leah gave a delighted screech, grabbed her son, and hugged him tight; Uncle Yaakov clapped him on the back.

"Well done!"

"Good for you, Yisrael David!"

"Gemarakup strikes again!"

When the congratulations were over and done with, Cousin Shmuel turned to him eagerly. "Where was he?" he asked. "And how did you figure it out?"

"The clue," Gemarakup grinned slyly, "was in the story that you didn't want to hear, and now I'll tell it."

Can you figure out where Benjy was, and how Gemarakup found him? [Turn to page 66 for the solution.]

VI.
The Chofetz Chaim Caper

O n those rare days when he didn't have too much homework to keep him busy, there was nothing Gemarakup enjoyed more than visiting Uncle Ezra's jewelry store, and having a talk with him. He enjoyed watching Uncle Ezra speak to the customers who came in looking for jewelry; was fascinated by Aryeh the watch repairman, who sat quietly in one corner of the store, his deft hand manipulating tiny tools; and was delighted to look at gems through Uncle Ezra's loupe, and seeing them appear, as if by magic, so clearly before his eye.

What he loved best, though, was talking about Uncle Ezra's special hobby — collecting old and rare *sefarim*. His uncle bought and sold the centuries-old books, keeping some of the treasures for his own extensive collection. Once in a while, he would let Gemarakup hold one of his precious acquisitions, and the boy would turn the pages of a three-hundred-year-old

Haggadah or century-old *Talmud,* marveling at the thoughts of the people who might have held the *sefer* in their hands before him.

One afternoon visit produced a special treat. As he and his uncle were enjoying a cup of hot chocolate, a man walked in and said, "Excuse me, Mr. Finkel, I've got a book that you might be interested in purchasing."

The man, who was not wearing a *yarmulka,* explained to Uncle Ezra that his uncle had recently passed away, leaving all

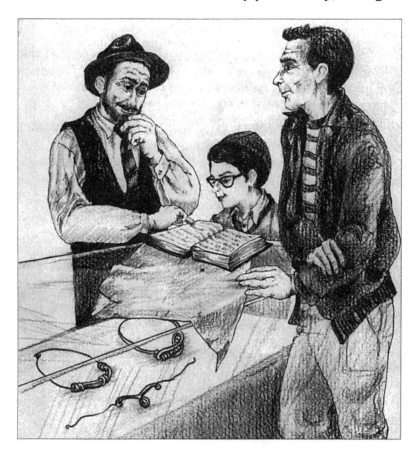

of his possessions to him, his only nephew. "Not that they amounted to much," the man, whose name was Mr. Atkins, said wryly. "Uncle Efram wasn't a rich man, and any money that he had, he put into his books. My uncle was very religious.

"I was going to donate his books to a local temple library," Mr. Atkins continued, "but a friend of mine who was helping me catalogue them, for tax purposes, you know, found one book that he thought might be valuable, and he suggested that I bring it to you for sale."

With this, Mr. Atkins pulled a small book, bound in a faded brown cover, out of his briefcase, and handed it to Ezra.

"Sefer Chofetz Chaim. Now let me see — printed in the year 5633 — why that makes this a first-edition copy! An original, sold by the Chofetz Chaim himself!"

Ezra turned to his nephew with growing excitement in his voice. "Can you imagine — the Chofetz Chaim himself handled this sefer! And in such good condition, too." He lovingly fingered the yellowed pages. "Why it's hardly been used — look here, some of the pages haven't even been cut."

"Well, it does my heart good to see someone who will appreciate Uncle Efram's legacy," said Mr. Atkins, smiling broadly. "I'm on my way out of the country for an extended business trip, and I've no time for haggling. Give me five hundred dollars for the book, and it's yours."

"Five hundred dollars," Ezra whispered to his nephew. "It's not much to pay, for such a work."

"It's five hundred dollars too much to pay for this," Gemarakup answered. "Don't give the man a cent. This book is a forgery!"

Can you figure out how Gemarakup knew that the sefer was a fake? [Turn to page 67 for the solution.]

VII.
The Mysterious
Disappearing Ball

here was considerable excitement in the yard of
Yeshiva Ahavas Chesed when Yossi Brown opened
his lunch box and drew out the birthday present he'd
received the day before from his parents.

"It's a glow-in-the-dark, high-flying, faster-than-the-speed-of-
light, incredible bouncer!" Yossi announced, waving the greenish-brown ball proudly in front of him.

Though, as Gemarakup noted dryly, the speed of the ball
did not approach that of the sun's rays, it *was* a fast, high-
bouncing one, and the sixth graders were soon pursuing it
excitedly through the schoolyard in a spirited game of catch.

Up it went, bouncing as high as the second floor windows, with a dozen boys scampering after it. When one of the boys would finally grab it, he would look desperately for a team member, and then throw it to him. If his partner missed the ball — there it would go, bouncing up and down, this way and that, with the boys again scampering wildly after it.

After fifteen minutes of furious play, Slugger found himself with the ball in hand and five "enemy" teammates coming after him. He looked around frantically, saw Gemarakup on the far side of the yard, and wildly pitched the ball with all his strength.

Gemarakup jumped up and reached, hands held high. The ball flew smoothly — two feet over his head. It bounced; up, up, up — and disappeared over the building.

With a great shout, the boys ran out; through the gate they went in pursuit of the ball. Yes, they knew that it was against the rules to leave the yard. But after all, this was a glow-in-the-dark, high-flying, faster-than-the-speed-of-light, incredible bouncer. And after a quarter of an hour spent chasing that kind of ball, no one was thinking too clearly... no one, that is, except...

Gemarakup and his friends raced around the corner, where the ball should have landed after flying over the school building, and stopped short. Right in front of them, coolly bouncing a greenish-brown ball against the school's front steps, was Akiva Stern!

While it might be exaggerating somewhat to call Akiva Stern a bully, it was true that in the years that Akiva had been in the *yeshiva,* he had gained renown as a boy whose brains were in his fists; the kind of guy who failed most of his tests and then sat on the students who had done well. No one liked him.

"Give me my ball," Yossi said to Akiva. "Your ball? This is my ball. I bought it myself, yesterday," Akiva replied nonchalantly, still bouncing the ball.

At this, there were shouts from the sixth graders: "Akiva stole it?" "Make Akiva give it back!" "Akiva is a crook!" and other such comments.

In their fury and frustration, no one noticed the thoughtful look that passed over Gemarakup's face; no one noticed him tap his friend Slugger on the shoulder; and no one noticed the two of them disappear.

When they returned a few moments later, though, they did notice. Gemarakup took a greenish-brown ball, identical to the one that Akiva was still bouncing, and threw it to Yossi. "I believe this is yours," he said with a grin.

Akiva stared, astounded. "How'd you find it, Gemarakup?" he finally asked.

"No problem, Akiva," Gemarakup answered. "The solution was clear — it was in your name."

Can you figure out how Gemarakup found the ball? [Turn to page 68 for the solution.]

VIII.
The Wild Drag Race

emarakup and his friends always chose the quiet route to walk on their way home from *shul* on *Shabbos* — it somehow felt more *"Shabbosdik."* The street was a residential one, shady, far from the roar of the business district. Only a few people could be seen: their fathers, following a few blocks behind them; some children playing on grassy lawns; an elderly woman crossing the street.

Suddenly the peace was shattered as two cars roared down the narrow street, one next to the other, speeding wildly — a drag race!

The horrified boys saw the two vehicles — a white Mustang, license number YD1525, and a red Volkswagen, URN 8105 —

careen down the street. The Volkswagen banged into a parked car, swerved to avoid a tree, and crashed into the elderly woman, who fell in a heap.

In seconds, as the boys watched in dismay, the cars disappeared, and the street was silent once again.

Gemarakup and his companions rushed to the side of the stricken woman, who lay moaning. "We've got to get help," he said urgently.

Slugger pointed to a lawn with a small sign blowing in the wind. "That's a doctor's office," he said, bounding toward it.

Within moments he reappeared, with a man in a white coat and holding a stethoscope following closely behind. The doctor gently examined the wounded woman. After a few moments, he instructed one of the people in the crowd that had gathered to go into his office and phone for an ambulance and a police car.

"She needs to be observed for a possible concussion, but she should be all right," he told the concerned onlookers. He turned to Gemarakup and his friends and said, "If you boys saw the accident, perhaps you'd better stay to speak to the police. The rest of you," he turned to the crowd, "should go home."

Soon, the wail of sirens again broke the serenity; the ambulance and the police had arrived. The woman, who had quietly told them that she had seen nothing at all of the car that had knocked her down, was quickly placed in the ambulance, which roared off.

A police officer, who introduced himself as Officer Kelly, questioned the boys; they told him what they'd seen.

"Ah, these drag racers," the officer sighed, shaking his head. "When will they ever learn?" He looked keenly at the youngsters standing before him. "None of you could identify the vehicles, I suppose?" he said.

Slugger, who took a keen interest in all matters dealing with cars, spoke up. "One of them was a late model Volkswagen, red; the other was a white Ford Mustang."

The police officer shrugged. "Not enough to go on. There's an awful lot of those cars driving around."

Gemarakup spoke up quietly. "What if I can give you their license numbers?" he said.

The policeman looked up alertly. "Oh, you wrote them down?" he asked. "That's a bright lad."

"No, today is our Sabbath, Officer Kelly, and we aren't even allowed to carry a pen," replied Gemarakup. "But I can tell you their license numbers anyway."

The policeman looked at him sternly. "Young man, don't try to be a hero. This is serious business. You're not going to convince me that you could see two license numbers in a split second, memorize them, and remember them after a full half hour, what with all the excitement that's gone on!"

Gemarakup smiled. "I think I can convince you, Officer," he said, "with only two words."

Can you figure out how Gemarakup remembered the numbers — and can you remember them too, without looking back? [Turn to page 69 for the solution.]

IX.
The Nighttime Break-in

t first they all thought it was the long-awaited color war "breakout." The lights went out, the camp was plunged into darkness. There were screams, shouts, giggles. Someone blew a whistle; the head counselor could be heard shouting that the boys should stay in their bunks.

Sternly warning the boys to stay put, Gemarakup's counselor, Yitzchak, left to find out what was happening. He returned a half hour later, just when the boys had reluctantly decided that color war was not on its way, and that this was, indeed, a real blackout.

"It seems that there's a major problem in a power plant nearby," Yitzchak told the eager boys. "Every camp in the mountains is without electricity."

A flurry of questions followed the news. "How long do you think it will last?" "Are the phones affected, too?" "Does the blackout go all the way to Brooklyn?" "Are you *sure* this isn't color war?"

"No one knows how long it will last," the counselor replied patiently, "but we expect to have electricity restored by morning. The phones are working, only this county has no power, and no — this is not a color war breakout!"

"If the electricity is out," Gemarakup remarked, thoughtfully, "the freezer won't be working."

"That's right!" exclaimed his bunkmate Yonasan. "And tomorrow night is *Rosh Chodesh!*"

In honor of *Rosh Chodesh Elul,* Camp Kayitz had prepared a special treat for the campers — luscious ice cream sundaes topped with whipped cream, chocolate syrup, and a maraschino cherry — served after *ma'ariv,* the evening prayers. But what was an ice cream sundae, if the ice cream was all melted?

"Don't worry," their counselor consoled them, "I've heard that if you don't open a freezer door, it stays cold for a long time. The stuff will stay frozen — I hope. Anyway, there's nothing we can do but get to bed."

The boys said *Shema* by the flickering beams of their flashlights. They finally settled down and went to sleep, amid gloomy thoughts of rivers of melted vanilla fudge ripple ice cream.

The next day dawned bright and clear. Gemarakup jumped out of bed and raced to the switch, flicked it — and then there was light. "End of power failure," he announced. "Everything's back to normal."

But everything was *not* back to normal. In the dining room after *davening,* as the boys downed their breakfast of French toast and syrup, they saw the camp director, who hardly ever came in during meals, hurriedly dash in and speak to the head counselor. The two men raced out the door together, leaving the boys agog with curiosity.

"Maybe it's got something to do with the ice cream," one of the boys suggested.

"I'll go and see," said their counselor, concerned over the fate of the vanilla-chocolate-strawberry.

He returned a few moments later, unsmiling. "Well?" the boys asked anxiously.

"Oh, the ice cream is okay," Yitzchak replied. "But something pretty mysterious has happened. A break-in, in the office."

Gemarakup jumped out of his seat. "Can I go help?" he asked.

The counselor shook his head. "They don't need any campers there," he said grimly.

Gemarakup sat down. His friend, Slugger, got up and whispered into the counselor's ear. Yitzchak looked at Gemarakup. "Okay, I didn't realize we had a super sleuth among us," he said with a smile. "You can go."

Gemarakup found a knot of people standing in front of the office. The director was explaining to the head counselor and division heads what had happened. "The robber knew that money was kept in the office, and, realizing that the alarm system wouldn't work because of the power failure, he simply opened the window from the outside and entered."

"Do you have any clues?" the head counselor asked.

"More than that, we have an eyewitness." The director motioned to a young man. "Joe, one of our gardening staff, says he saw the whole thing."

"I sure did," said the heavy-set man with the thick black eyebrows and stubbly chin. "I saw it clearly. I was standing outside smoking — I don't like to smoke indoors — and I saw someone climb out of the window, carrying a green bag."

"That's where the money was kept," the director interjected.

"It was dark out, but by the light of the moon I could see the guy's face. And that's why I didn't think much of it — you see, I thought he had some business in the office. It was Jake that I saw. It was only this morning that I heard about the robbery, and realized that Jake was the thief."

There was only one Jake in camp; Jake Schwartz, camp driver and handyman. He was a genial fellow, universally liked by all the boys.

At that moment the handyman himself appeared at a run. Joe took a step towards him. "There he is," he said. "That's the one who did it! I seen it with my own two eyes!"

"Saw what?" Jake asked. "I heard that there was a robbery last night."

The group stared wordlessly at him. Finally, the director spoke. "Where were you last night, Jake?" he asked.

"Why, sleeping. In my room."

"Can you prove it?"

"Well, no. I sleep by myself, you know. But what's going on?"

"Someone has accused you of theft, Jake."

The handyman stared. "Me? But I didn't ... I couldn't ... I never..."

Suddenly, Gemarakup's voice came through, loud and clear. "Don't worry, Jake, you didn't do it. Joe is lying."

The heavy-set man turned on him. "You saying I didn't see the thief, boy?" he snarled.

"Oh, you saw him all right — when you looked in the mirror this morning." He turned to the camp director. "Jake is innocent — and I can prove it."

Can you figure out how Gemarakup knew who was innocent, and who was guilty? [Turn to page 71 for the solution.]

X.
The Ellis Island Calamity

hen you leave things for the last minute, they don't
always work out. They didn't, that Monday afternoon, for Gemarakup and his best friend Slugger.

It had been a busy week — a major test on *Chumash*, the
Mishnayos be'al peh contest finals, and sandlot baseball every
evening. A crowded week, a busy week: a week in which the
boys somehow never found the time to put together a report
that Mr. Jacobs, their social studies teacher, had assigned.

They weren't too worried about the project, a joint report
on Ellis Island, the port of entry through which hundreds of

thousands of Eastern European Jews had passed and where they had caught their first glimpse of America. After all, it wouldn't take more than an hour in the library, checking encyclopedias. So what if they had waited until the very last day before it was due?

And so they found themselves, on that Monday afternoon, staring with dismay at the hand-lettered sign in the library window: "Library closed for emergency repairs, due to flood in basement."

Disaster.

"Maybe your mom can drive us to another branch," suggested Slugger. His own father, he knew, commuted to work, and so his car wouldn't be available until after the libraries had all closed.

They rushed to the nearest public telephone. "I'm sorry, dear, but *Abba* took the car to the mechanic for repairs," his mother told Gemarakup. "Besides, you've got to pick up Tamar and walk her home."

Gloomily, Gemarakup made his way to the nursing home where his younger sister was waiting. Some months before, Tamar had begun visiting the elderly invalids as part of a *chesed* project run by her school. She'd been so touched by the gratitude of the old people, and she had learned so much from them that she had decided to continue her weekly visits even after the project had come to an end. For a long time she'd been after her brother to join her, but he never found the time.

As they walked towards home, Gemarakup told Tamar of his problem.

"So you've got no report to hand in," she mused aloud.

"Yeah, and Mr. Jacobs is going to kill us. He hates kids who are late with reports," Gemarakup moaned. "And we did have a whole week to do it!"

"Well, maybe you can break it to him gently," Tamar suggested.

"Gently," replied her brother, with a touch of sarcasm in his voice. "Like Serach bas Asher, who walked around singing 'Yosef is alive,' so that Yaakov wouldn't be too shocked at the news. Sure," he laughed, "all we have to do is go around tomorrow singing, 'Our report is late.' That's a great idea, Tamar."

Suddenly Gemarakup stopped short. "Wait a minute! Tamar — that is a great idea. Of course — Serach bas Asher — that's the answer to our problem!"

Swiftly, he whirled around and began to walk rapidly in the direction from which they'd just come. Then he stopped at a telephone booth just long enough to call Slugger. "C'mon, we've no time to lose!" he cried to his astonished friend. "We've got a report to do! Bring your notebook and some pens and meet me at ..."

Can you figure out where Gemarakup told Slugger to meet him, and how they will complete their assignment? [Turn to page 72 for the solution.]

XI.

The Curious Case
of the Cackling Coop

"Yisrael David," called Mrs. Finkel. In a flash, Gemarakup promptly appeared before her. "How would you like to do a *mitzvah,* and have an interesting week besides?"

"Sure, *Imma,*" he answered eagerly. After all, he was always happy to do a *mitzvah* — and this week at home, with camp over and school not yet begun, had been rather dull.

"Your Uncle Marcel has been called away on business, leaving *Tante* Pearl stuck alone on the farm. Would you go, together with Tamar, to keep her company and give her a hand?"

"Would I? Just give me five minutes to pack!"

"You can have a little more time than that," laughed his mother. "You can leave on the first train tomorrow."

And so it was that brother and sister found themselves on the Pennsylvania-bound express train. Both were excited: They loved their mother's aunt, *Tante* Pearl, and always enjoyed their trips to the chicken farm where she and Uncle Marcel lived. This was the first time that they would be staying there for a long visit. Gemarakup, particularly, looked forward to trying out life as a farmer.

Immediately after a most delicious dinner, *Tante* Pearl took her enthusiastic great-nephew to the huge aluminum-roofed chicken coop. Gemarakup saw row after row after row of cages, with chickens sitting two or three to a cage. At the bottom of each cage was a bin for the eggs that the hens laid.

"We've got 2,000 chickens," *Tante* Pearl remarked, as she showed Gemarakup how to take each egg and place it in a cardboard box. "And each one lays an egg every second day or so."

It didn't take long for Gemarakup to figure out the mathematics of it — 1,000 eggs a day to be gathered and sorted! And it didn't take long for him to realize that egg farming was not all that it was cracked up to be: Gathering eggs was dull, tedious work!

After two interminable stretches of work, Gemarakup ventured to suggest to his sister that she try her hand at it, but Tamar was unenthusiastic. "I've got to think of something," he said to himself, as he moved slowly from cage to cage.

"Wait! I've got it!" he shouted aloud, almost dropping a dozen eggs in his excitement. He smiled at no one in particular, and then cheerfully told a snow-white hen: "This is the last time I'll be bothering you. I'm going to take a hint from an Arab king, no less!"

The next day, and the next, and the one after that, Tamar carefully gathered all the eggs in the coop, while her brother read a book in the sunshine.

> **Can you figure out how Gemarakup got his sister to do his job? [Turn to page 73 for the solution.]**

The Solutions

I. The Unlucky Dreidel

Gemarakup Solves the Mystery

"A story about our *gedolim* gives us the solution for the case," said Gemarakup.

Slugger groaned. "Not another one of his endless stories," he thought to himself.

Gemarakup gave him a disapproving look and continued:

❧ ❧ ❧

Many years ago, we are told, an honest butcher lived in a small *shtetl* in Europe. Next to his butcher store, separated from it by only a thin partition, was the shop of a grocer.

Each night, the honest butcher would take the few coins he had earned that day and hide them in a little hole beneath the stone floor.

One night, he lifted the stone to hide the day's earnings, and, to his horror, he found that his coins were all gone!

"The grocer next door must have seen me put my money away. No one else knows of my hiding place," he thought.

The next morning, he angrily entered the neighboring shop to find the grocer greedily counting a pile of coins.

"Those are mine! Give them back!" he shouted.

"I am an honest man," replied the grocer. "These are my hard-earned coins, and you are trying to steal them from me!"

The butcher was brokenhearted. He made his way to the *Rav* to tell him what had happened and to ask his advice. The

Rav thought for a moment, and then, with the butcher following him, strode into the grocer's store.

"You want to prove that these coins belong to you, don't you?" he asked the grocer. The man nodded.

"Let us, then, do a simple test. Bring me a pail of water," he ordered.

The puzzled grocer did as he was told. The *Rav* took the coins and dropped them into the pail!

"Now," said the *Rav*, "as you can see, the coins drop to the bottom. But if you look carefully at the water, you will see drops of grease floating on the water. Since a butcher works with fatty meat all day long, his fingers would be slick with fat — and so would the coins he handles. But a grocer and his coins would not be greasy! This proves that the coins belong to the butcher!"

The grocer, dismayed, admitted his guilt, and returned the money.

❧ ❧ ❧

"Now," said Gemarakup, "we have just enjoyed a very good — and very oily — meal of *latkes*. Only Chezky, who is allergic to fried foods, had nothing greasy. If we put the *dreidel* into the water, and oily bubbles rise to the top, that means that the *dreidel* must belong to the one who ate the *latkes* — Slugger. But if the water remains clear, why, it must belong to the only one with clean, non-greasy hands — Chezky!"

With a flourish, Gemarakup dropped the *dreidel* into the cup. Everyone, even Chezky, watched as bubbles of oil slowly floated to the top.

"Well, boys, it seems to me that someone owes someone an apology — and a *dreidel*," said Gemarakup quietly.

Chezky, his face as red as the *dreidel* that he handed to Slugger, said, "I guess Ephraim did switch them around. I'm sorry."

"That's okay, Chezky," replied Slugger. "I've got the *dreidel* back; no harm done." He turned to Gemarakup. "From *talmid chacham* to detective," he said with a laugh. "Not bad, Gemarakup."

Gemarakup smiled. "It was the *Rav* who solved the mystery," he said.

II. The Great Jewel Robbery
Gemarakup Finds the Diamond

"I realized where the diamond was hidden because of a story from the *Gemara* that my *rebbe* just told the class," said Gemarakup.

❈ ❈ ❈

Two men were having an argument. One claimed that he'd lent the other money which had not yet been repaid; the other claimed that he'd returned it. They took their quarrel to the *Beis Din,* the Rabbinical court. The judge, knowing that the man would be afraid to swear falsely, ordered the borrower to swear that he had returned the loan.

When they asked him to swear, the borrower asked the lender to hold his walking stick for him while he took the oath. The lender did so, and the borrower swore that he had returned the loan.

The lender was furious, because he knew the man was lying. In a rage, he took the man's walking stick and threw it violently to the ground. It broke in two, and money — the exact amount that the man had borrowed — rolled out! The borrower had been afraid to swear falsely and so he had cleverly hidden the coins in the stick that the lender would hold while he pronounced the oath. What he swore was true. He had given the coins back, although the lender wasn't aware of that!

❧ ❧ ❧

"When we were watching the videotape," Gemarakup continued, "I noticed something very strange. Why was the young man in the store carrying an umbrella if this entire week has been warm and sunny?

"I am sure that man is an accomplice, and he used his umbrella in the same way that the man in the *Gemara* used his walking stick — to hide the diamond. And if you're lucky, he'll be so pleased with his hiding place that he will simply leave it there until the police have given up the search."

The detective scratched his head. "A clue in a kid's story? It sounds unlikely to me. Still, it was a sunny day, and it can't hurt to follow the lead."

And so the police took out a search warrant, checked the man's home, and found that Gemarakup's "kid story" had led them to the diamond!

III. The Bad-Tempered Kohein
Gemarakup Stops a Fight

"I got the idea for ending the fight from the boys' names. People with the names of Cohen and Katz are usually *Kohanim*.

"We learned today that one of the differences between a *Kohein* and a *Yisrael*, even now, is in the area of *gittin*, divorce. You see, unlike a *Yisrael*, a *Kohein* is not allowed to marry a divorcee, even if she had been his wife previously.

"Therefore, when a *get* is written for a *Kohein*, the parchment is specially prepared, in a way that takes a long time. The *chachamim* thought that this would give a short-tempered *Kohein* a chance to cool off, and not give a divorce. That way he would not create a situation which he would later regret and be unable to change.

"I tried to do the same thing — give those two hot-tempered *Kohanim* something to do, so they would have a chance to cool off! I made them run around, so that they wouldn't have time to ask me what I was doing. In the interval, they realized that their fight was silly."

"Great idea," said Slugger admiringly. "How'd you think of it so fast?"

"It just comes from listening in class," said Gemarakup. "You should try doing that more often," he added with a smile.

IV. The Hungry Hoodlums

Gemarakup Uncovers a Lie

"Sit down, fellows, and I'll tell you a little story," said Gemarakup softly to the four surly boys.

❈ ❈ ❈

Hundreds of years ago, two men came to a great Jewish sage, Rabbi Moshe Isserles, whom we call the Rama.

One of the men claimed that the other had stolen a bag of gold coins from him. They had been walking together, he claimed, and, when they had reached a well, he had asked his companion to hold his bag of coins while he took a drink. When he was finished, he asked for the return of his bag, but the man denied ever having received a bag of coins!

The other man told the Rama that the entire story — the well, the bag of coins, everything — was a figment of his fellow traveler's imagination.

The Rama thought for a moment, and then told the man who claimed that he'd been robbed, "Go back to the well, and bring me a cup of water. That water has magical powers, and will be able to show me who is telling the truth."

The man agreed and left immediately. The suspect, laughing to himself, thought, "How silly. Water has no magic powers."

A few hours went by before the Rama turned to the suspect. "Your companion must be lost," he said. "It shouldn't take so long to get to the well from here."

"Oh, no, he's not lost," answered the man. "It's at least a two-hour journey to the well."

"Oh! So there was a well after all," said the Rama. "And yet, you denied it. You must be lying — and now you must return the money."

※ ※ ※

"I borrowed an idea from the Rama," Gemarakup continued, "and used your own tongue to trick you. You claim that you haven't been in the neighborhood of our school for weeks, and yet you know about the construction project that just began this evening. Obviously, you are lying and are the guilty ones!"

The sergeant stood up and faced the culprits. "Well?" he said.

The leader of the gang shrugged. "Okay, we did it," he said. "But who'd've thought that a creepy little kid would be the one to find us out?"

Gemarakup smiled. "Oh no! It was no 'creepy little kid'," he said. "It was the Rama."

V. The Terror of Teaneck

Gemarakup Finds the Lost Child

"This is the story that gave me the clue," said Gemarakup.

❀ ❀ ❀

Our *gedolim* in Europe often grew up in severe poverty. They ate little, dressed in clothes that were more like rags, and often had no home but their *beis midrash*. And yet, they would still persevere and learn, and be concerned for others.

One of the *gedolim* who was materially deprived in his youth was the Steipler *Gaon*. When he was still young, learning in the *yeshiva* in Bialystok, he would often give up his bed to someone who needed it, he thought, more than he, and he would spend the night on the hard wooden benches of the *beis midrash*.

He slept there one winter night. In the morning, when the people came to *daven,* they didn't notice the tired young man lying on the bench, and they put their coats over him. It was, he later said, the warmest and best sleep he ever had there!

❀ ❀ ❀

"Well," continued Gemarakup, "I thought, if I were a three-year-old looking for a warm, quiet place to sleep off my vodka, I would want to be covered with coats like the Steipler was! And so I checked under the pile of coats on Yosh's bed — and there he was — our little *talmid chacham*."

Everyone laughed, and the Terror of Teaneck opened his eyes, smiled, and went happily back to sleep.

VI. The Chofetz Chaim Caper

Gemarakup Spots a Forgery

"Perhaps you didn't know this, Mr. Atkins," Gemarakup told the astonished man, "but one of the things the author of the *Sefer Chofetz Chaim* was renowned for was his unflinching honesty in business dealings.

"He was always afraid of shortchanging his customers, of selling them something defective, or of not giving them their money's worth. And so, before he put a *sefer* up for sale, he or a member of his family scrupulously checked every single page. They cut each page, and made absolutely certain that everything was printed properly.

"As soon as I saw that there were uncut pages, I realized the truth: This book never passed through the hands of the Chofetz Chaim. And, I might add, I suspect it never even passed through the hands of any Uncle Efram."

Atkins glared at the boy and stuffed the book back into his briefcase.

"If you're thinking of peddling that book elsewhere, just remember that I am friendly with all the local book dealers," Uncle Ezra told the red-faced man. "And I'll be certain to mention today's incident."

"And Mr. Atkins," Ezra continued, as the man hurried out, "perhaps you ought to read some of the Chofetz Chaim's works. His discussion of honesty and business ethics might be of particular interest to you."

VII. The Mysterious Disappearing Ball

Gemarakup Finds the High-Flyer

"Your name, Akiva," said Gemarakup, "gave me the clue. It reminded me of a story."

❊ ❊ ❊

Rabbi Akiva, though always a very moral man, was, as a youth, totally ignorant. Why, he didn't even know the *aleph-beis.*

And then, when he was forty years old and had despaired of ever learning anything, he noticed a rock upon which water dripped steadily. The water, dripping drop by drop, had worn down a deep hole in the rock.

"Surely, if drops of water can wear down a hard rock," the unlearned Rabbi Akiva thought, "the Torah, which is compared to water, will be able to penetrate even my heart!" He began to study, and ultimately became the Torah giant of his generation, and one of the greatest scholars in our history.

❀ ❀ ❀

"Well, the idea of water made me think: If the ball went over the building, and didn't bounce down on the other side, it could very well have fallen in the drain pipe near the roof of the building. And so, with a chair and a boost from Slugger, I was able to find the missing ball."

Akiva gazed at Gemarakup. "He was forty years old when he started to learn Torah, you say! And he became so great?"

Gemarakup nodded. Akiva casually flipped his ball to him. "Here, you can play with this for the rest of lunch hour," he said. "I've got some homework that I didn't get around to doing last night. Maybe I'll take a look at it, after all." Just as casually, Gemarakup flipped the ball to Slugger. "If you don't mind, Akiva, maybe I'll see if I can lend you a hand," he said, and smiled.

And together the two boys walked away.

VIII. The Wild Drag Race

Gemarakup Plays a Numbers Game

"The two words," said Gemarakup, "are love — and animals!"

The policeman gave him an odd look and he quickly continued, "No, Officer Kelly, I'm not teasing. You see, when I saw the accident, I realized that the license numbers were important, and quickly made note of them. But, like you, I realized that without writing them down, I might very well get confused, and so I turned to an ancient Jewish practice.

"You see, one of the ways of interpreting our holy works is through the system which we call *gematria*. Each of the letters of the Hebrew alphabet is equivalent to a number: the first letter, *aleph*, is one; the second, *beis*, two; and so on. We examine the words of our Torah and look for significance in their numerical value.

"I immediately tried converting the license numbers into words, by seeing the numbers as letters, because it is much simpler to remember a word than a random series of numbers. I was lucky," Gemarakup grinned, "because each of the license numbers turned out to be an easily remembered word."

He took a deep breath and went on, "One car carried the number YD 1525; the other was URN 8105.

"The YD was easy — my name is Yisrael David, and those are my initials. The numbers 1-5-2-5, in Hebrew letters, are *aleph, hei, beis, hei* — which spells *ahavah*, or love — something that the driver lacked completely.

"The other license plate was even more interesting. The numbers 8-10-5, spell out *ches, yud, hei* — or *chayah*, animal. Read together with the letters, you have 'U-R-N (you are an) animal' — which is really a fitting description of people who endanger others."

The police officer looked at Gemarakup. "Are you sure about this, son?" he said, scratching his head.

Gemarakup's father replied for him. "I'm confident that my son transposed the numbers into the correct letters," he assured the officer.

"Well, we'll run a computer check on cars with those licenses, and if they match the description, then — their goose is cooked!" the policeman said.

Gemarakup smiled. "Cooked goose reminds me that we've got a hot plate of *cholent* waiting for us at home!"

And off they went.

IX. The Nighttime Break-in
Gemarakup Traps a Thief

"Joe here claims he saw Jake break in," Gemarakup told the astonished men standing around him. "He claims he saw it all so clearly that he could even tell the color of the bag the money was kept in.

"Joe must have terrific eyesight, making out colors and faces on a night when all the lights went out."

"I told you, I saw it all by the light of the moon," Joe broke in.

Gemarakup ignored the interruption. "Joe's terrific eyesight is matched only by his imagination. He saw the entire robbery by the light of the moon — on the evening before *Rosh Chodesh*."

He turned to the dumbfounded man. "You see, the Jewish calendar is a lunar one, based on the moon's appearance in the sky. *Rosh Chodesh,* the beginning of the new month, falls on the night when the moon first appears in the sky. On the night before *Rosh Chodesh* there is never any trace of the moon to be seen!

"There was no electricity, no moonlight — and no Jake. But there was a thief carrying a green bag full of money, and it must have been you."

The camp director stared at the sullen man. "You have five minutes to return the cash and pack your bags," he said quietly. "Or else I'll call the police."

Joe put his hand into his pocket and pulled out a roll of bills. "It's all here," he said. Then he turned on his heels and disappeared.

The director faced Jake and said, "I suspected you falsely. I publicly ask for your forgiveness."

The embarrassed handyman shrugged. "Of course," he muttered. "No hard feelings."

The grateful director then turned to Gemarakup, who was on his way back to the dining room. "And as for you, Yisrael David, how can I thank you?"

The boy smiled. "Chocolate chip is my favorite flavor," he laughed.

X. The Ellis Island Calamity
Gemarakup Completes the Report

Gemarakup and Slugger met at the nursing home that Tamar had been visiting. When Slugger arrived, Gemarakup told his friend about his plan:

❁ ❁ ❁

When the time had come for Israel to leave Egypt, everybody was busy getting gold and silver from their former masters. Everybody, except for Moshe *Rabbeinu*. He was searching for the remains of Yosef. They had been destined to be brought out of Egypt at the time of the Redemption for burial in *Eretz Yisrael*. Thus it had been promised centuries before.

But Moshe had a problem. He had no idea where Yosef's remains were hidden. He thought and thought, and finally turned to Serach — the daughter of Yosef's brother Asher — who was still alive. And sure enough, Serach was able to tell him that the Egyptians had hidden Yosef's remains in the Nile, both in the hope that in Yosef's merit the waters would be blessed and because they felt sure that Israel would never leave without the remains.

❦ ❦ ❦

"Well," said Gemarakup, "we can do the same thing — go to someone elderly, who can tell us the truth about how things were in the past. I'm sure, Tamar, that someone in your nursing home passed through Ellis Island."

"Of course!" shouted Tamar. "Mrs. Berkowitz! She's told me all about her days as an immigrant, and I think she came through Ellis Island."

And so, everyone got what they wanted: Mr. Jacobs got his assignment, on time; Gemarakup and Slugger got an A + for a "very special and creative project"; Mrs. Berkowitz got three extra visitors — and Gemarakup, after meeting Tamar's elderly friend, got the best reward of all: He began to join his sister on her regular visits to the nursing home.

XI. The Curious Case of the Cackling Coop

Gemarakup Learns a Lesson

Uncle Marcel returned from his trip on Friday afternoon. Everyone was busy with *Shabbos* preparations, and there was little time for talk. *Shabbos* passed quickly; they *davened* in the small *shul* nearby, and had wonderful *Shabbos* meals with lilting *zemiros* and interesting *divrei Torah.*

It was only after *havdalah* that Uncle Marcel was able to chat with his grandnephew about the week's work.

"So, Yisrael David, what do you think of chicken farming, now that you've gotten to know it first hand?" he asked his nephew.

"I'll tell you the truth, Uncle. I like my eggs fried or scrambled," said Gemarakup with a laugh. "As a matter of fact, I got Tamar to do the gathering for most of the week."

Uncle Marcel gazed at him. "And how'd you manage that, my boy? I've been trying to get *Tante* Pearl to do it for forty years now, and haven't succeeded!"

"You see, Uncle, I remembered a story, a legend of how the *Kosel Hama'aravi* was unearthed."

❀ ❀ ❀

It was hundreds of years ago, and the *Kosel,* the last remnant of our *Beis Hamikdash,* lay lost under the heaps of garbage that the non-Jews had dumped upon it for centuries.

Sultan Salim heard rumors of a holy place that was buried, and he resolved to uncover it. But how?

He came up with a brilliant scheme. He scattered gold coins throughout the area where he knew the Wall to be. Then he invited the poor people to come and get the coins.

Over 10,000 of them came, burrowing, moving heaps of garbage to find the coins. And slowly, slowly, the Wall appeared. And thus the *Kosel* was uncovered!

❀ ❀ ❀

"I thought of this story," Gemarakup said, "because I, too, needed something picked up. So I told Tamar that I would hide a few presents — some gum, candy, a little toy or two — under the eggs. We made a game of it. I hid the 'treasures,' and she found them, by gathering eggs!

"A good idea — worthy of a sultan, isn't it, Uncle?" Gemarakup finished proudly.

His uncle looked searchingly at him, was still for a moment, and then spoke. "Let me tell you a story, another one about the same Wall," he said.

※ ※ ※

When the *Beis Hamikdash* was being rebuilt, there was great excitement among the people; everyone wanted to do something. The rich merchants got together and raised enormous sums of money to buy marvelous building equipment. They had huge throngs of slaves build the magnificent walls at their expense. And so it was with the wealthy businessmen, and the prosperous farmers, and all who had money.

But the poor people, too, wished to have a share in this Holy Temple. Lacking funds for slaves, they themselves labored at one wall, building it on their own time, with their own muscles, their own sweat.

It is told that *Hashem* looked down upon these perspiring, impoverished workers, who somehow found the time and energy and strength to go and work for Him, and said, "All the other walls shall one day be destroyed, but this wall is dearest to Me, and will stand eternally." That wall was the *Kosel Hama'aravi,* which still stands today.

※ ※ ※

Gemarakup's uncle looked sternly at him. "Do you understand what I am trying to tell you, Yisrael David?"

Yisrael David hung his head in shame. "I guess ... I suppose I could have earned the *mitzvah* of *chesed* by gathering the eggs myself, instead of 'selling' the *mitzvah* for a few pieces of gum. Then it really would have been my *mitzvah*."

His great-uncle smiled. "Don't feel badly, my boy. If you've learned the lesson, this has been a week well spent. And besides, you're not leaving until tomorrow afternoon. We've still got tomorrow morning to gather those eggs. Will you give me a hand?"

"You bet!" shouted Gemarakup.